03/24
STAND PRICE
$ 5.00

Alison and Her RAINY DAY ROBOT

by Fred Chao

Alison and Her Rainy Day Robot
by Fred Chao

Published by Fred Chao

ISBN 978-0-615-76340-8

Letters: Jesse Post
Design: Fred Chao

First Printing, May 2013
Printed in Mexico

For Katherine,

sorry I beat up on you so much,
but hey, at least we were never bored

Bored.

Bored bored bored.

Bored bored bored bored bored bored bored.

It's a rainy day and Alison doesn't know what to do.

She is just so —

AAAuUUGHH!

I'm so BORED!

Hmph!

Alison has already played with her dolls.

She's played Tea Time with her stuffed animals.

She's even done her homework!

She wants something to do.

I know!

DING!

So Alison runs to the closet . . .

. . . and lets out the penguins!

And her monkey friend, Andrew.

So Alison and the penguins and her monkey friend Andrew start drawing out blueprints for the robot.

They work very hard.

Who knew that even the *planning* would take so much effort?

wak

Great! You found the supplies!

So now they can start building!

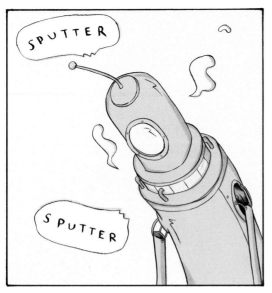

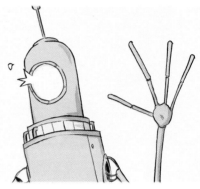

It worked! Alison couldn't be happier.
Her robot actually worked!

So Alison and her friends start cleaning up.

I think this belt looks pretty good on me.

⁝wak⁝

Okay, okay. I'll put it away.

That goes in the basement.

Crayons go in the drawer. Research books go on the shelf.

This is my least favorite part of cleaning.

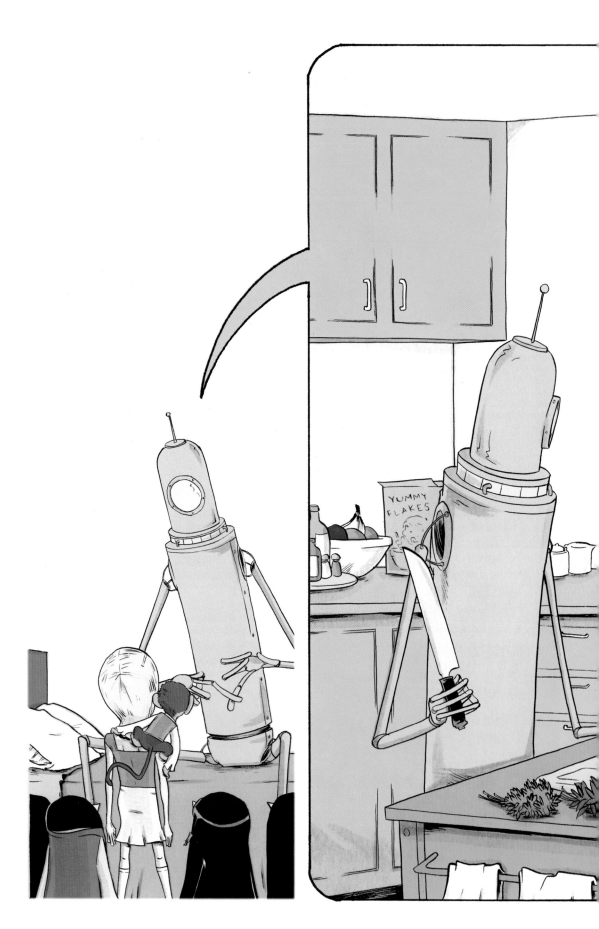

A gazpacho is a traditional Spanish dish, kind of like a cold tomato soup. We put tomatoes, cucumber, bell peppers, celery, and olive oil in a blender and put it in the refrigerator. Then we can eat it in an hour!

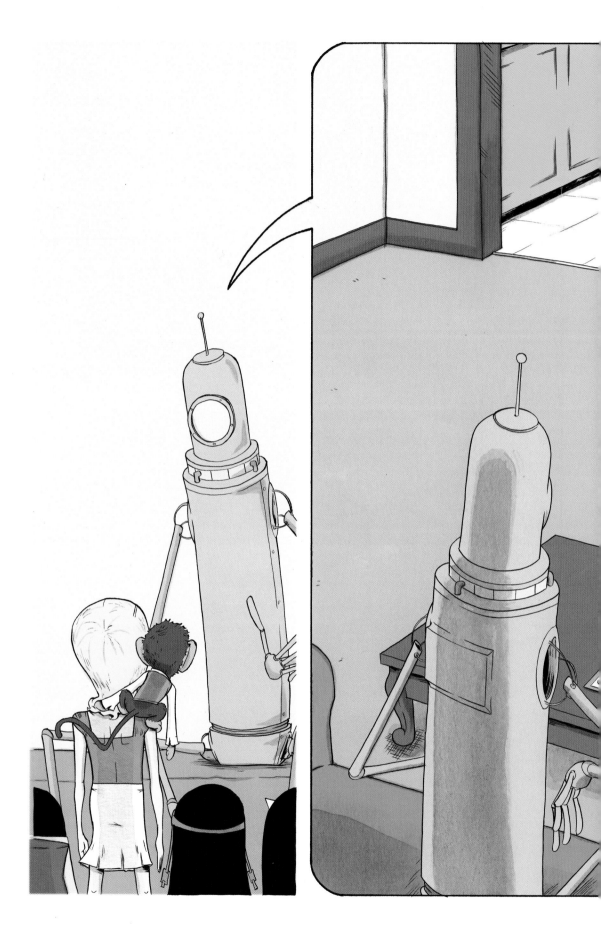

Chess is a boring game! I don't like chess!

Actually, Alison didn't like chess because she often lost to Andrew. After a while, she just became a sore loser.

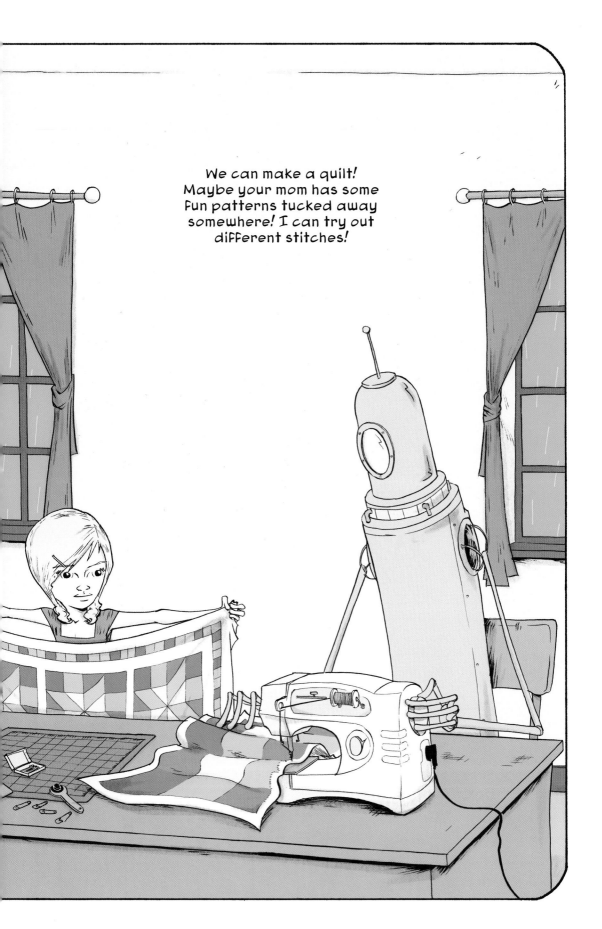

You're . . . you're right. I shouldn't blame you.

It's just . . . I got so excited, and I ended up expecting too much from you.

I'm . . . I'm sorry I got mad and yelled.

They looked at each other. Neither of them said a word.

The only sound was that of the rain.

And so . . .

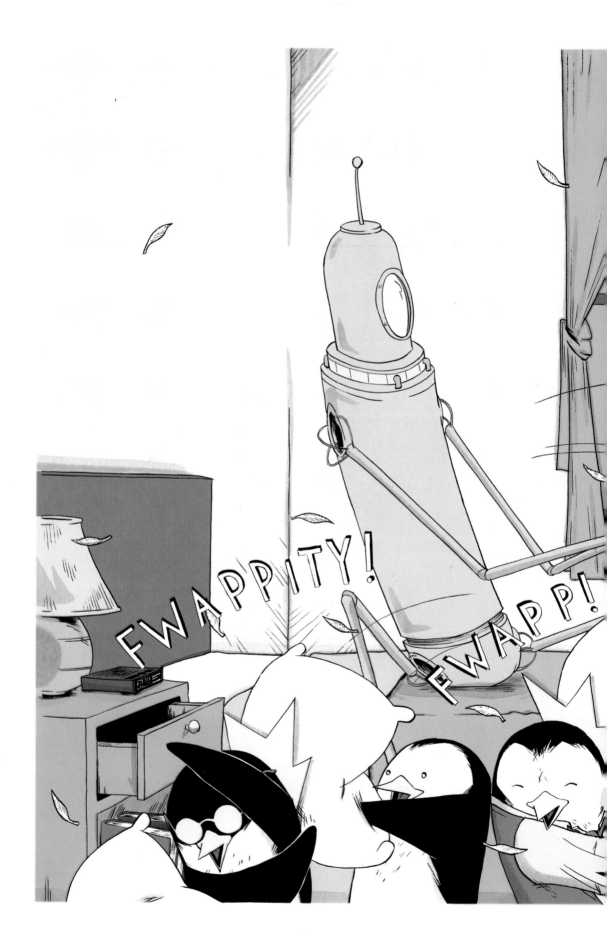

56

. . . ZZZ . . .

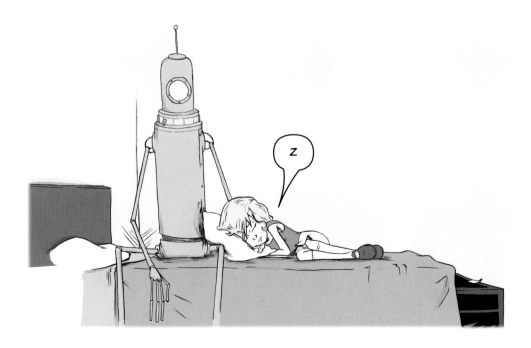

FRED CHAO is the writer and illustrator of *Johnny Hiro {Half Asian, All Hero}*, parts of which appeared in *The Best American Comics 2010*.

His comics have also appeared in *Found: Requiem for a Paper Bag*.

He was born in 1978 in San Francisco, California, and recently moved back to the Bay Area. He misses Brooklyn terribly.